LOVE'S LITURGY

By FORREST L. INGRAM

For you, Michele,
Forrest

Edited by Forrest & Ann Ingram

Forrest L. Ingram Publisher
Chicago, IL USA

Love's Liturgy
by Forrest L. Ingram

First Printing – February 2012
ISBN: 978-1-60047-664-8
Library of Congress Control Number: 2011942841

Printed in the U.S.A.

0   1   2   3   4   5   6   7   8   9

Dedication

To the love of my life,

my one and only—

Ann Ingram

and

in loving memory of my parents

Herschel and Vivian Ingram

and

Ad Majorem Dei Gloriam

PREFACE

True love is like a religion. For a lover, the loved one is a kind of "god" or "goddess." The language lovers use in speaking to and about one another is remarkably similar to the language used by devoted worshippers of a Supreme Being. True lovers may "adore" or "idolize" one another, experience "ecstasy" in one another's presence, "contemplate" or "be transported by" one another's beauty, and "be ruled" by one another's desires. They "give" or "devote" their lives to one another. Their lives have no "meaning" without the other.

What surprise could there be, then, that lovers, like religious devotees, create "days to remember" in their histories with one another? Just as religious communities create liturgical feasts to celebrate events in which the Supreme Power showed them how much He loves them—for example, by leading them out through the Red Sea, or by raising the Son of God from the dead—so too do lovers remember the first date, the first kiss, the first night they joined their bodies in sacred love-making, the day they officially swore that their union would be eternal.

Every religion has its liturgies to celebrate its special feast days. It is natural, therefore, that lovers too should create their own liturgies to celebrate their love life. The poems in this book, while covering the entire year, focus primarily on four specific celebrations of the lovers Forrest and Ann Ingram.

Every pair of lovers has its own feasts. Perhaps these poems may stimulate all lovers to treasure their own special feasts and to celebrate them in their own special way.

Wine and Roses

INTRODUCTION

Background:

When Forrest was the chairman of the English Department at Roosevelt University, Ann who was an English major received a letter from the University indicating that she had to meet with Forrest Ingram if she wanted to complete her degree.[1] For some reason, his name disturbed her. Why? No name ever had. She imagined a gargoyle with a foreboding expression on his face. It caused her to pace and to ponder.

She made an appointment to meet with this formidable chairman of English. She stood at the door and peeked in. Forrest was on the phone, leaning back in his chair with his feet on the desk. He was not a gargoyle. Tension drained out of her, immediately. Whatever she had feared dissipated. She sighed in relief, sure that she could "deal" with him.

When Forrest saw her at the door, he removed his feet from the desk. A blush colored his cheeks. He noticed that she was gorgeous, but gave no indication that he had been impressed by her beauty. In a few moments, he had finished his call and so invited her in.

She showed him her transcripts and held her breath. He rummaged through them without showing any reaction. He noticed an "A" here, and an "F" there. In fact, there did not seem to be anything but A's and F's in her records. (He did not immediately think: "Ann and Forrest.")

She explained her tendency to ignore what she did not find interesting, and her enthusiasm for exciting literature. She did not

---

[1] Ann was far from being a conventional student: in her first three years in college, when she was in a class, if she enjoyed what was being taught, she focused on it and aced the course. Her professors gave her high marks (A's) and delighted in her insightful comments and her artful expressions of ideas. Her memory astounded them. But if she did not care for the subject or the particular material being presented, she ignored it. She half-read the texts and gave half-hearted attention to them. The professors reflected their opinions in her grades (F's). By coincidence, those are the initials of Ann and Forrest.

need many more credits to finish her degree. He counseled her, told her what courses he would be teaching, and ended the session. At the doorway, she turned, looked at him, and said "I'll be back." She later admitted that she had never said "I'll be back" to any other man.

She enrolled in his seminar on "Literature, Justice, and the Law." Each session lasted three hours, with a break in the middle. During the break, they would sometimes go get coffee or a cold drink. So they had a few moments here and there to talk about things other than the readings for class.

As the class went on, Ann learned a lot and was deeply impressed by what Forrest had to say. When speaking with others, she would often start a sentence with: "There's this guy Forrest Ingram . . ." and then go on to remark about anything and everything.

While teaching, Forrest attended law school at night. Before Ann obtained her degree, Forrest told Ann that he would be leaving the University to begin a career in law. Ann responded: "What am I supposed to do without you?" Forrest replied: "Annie, I'll always be there for you." A bond had been growing between them, although they had never had a date or crossed any line of propriety.

During the next few years, Ann was pursuing her private life with various boyfriends, husbands, and lovers. She would call Forrest from time to time to meet him for lunch. Then she noticed that she was spending an inordinate amount of time deciding what to wear for such meetings. Deep down, she knew that she would not be agonizing over such choices if she did not have an interest in Forrest that exceeded the interest of a former student in a former teacher. So she kept cancelling her appointments with him.

When Ann first met Forrest, both were married. Ann, however, was on the verge of a divorce. After her divorce was finalized, she flew away to Florida to live with a man she knew there. Later, she married a high-powered attorney in New York and went to live with him there.

In her conversations with her New York husband, she would often inject: "There's this guy Forrest Ingram . . ." and continue with whatever topic was on the table. He noticed and said to her:

"Now, Ann, he was much more to you than just a teacher." As time passed, she had to admit to herself that he was right.

Five weeks into their marriage, her New York husband experienced a ruptured aorta and collapsed in Ann's arms. She grabbed him and held him, with sudden exceptional strength and perseverance, and so prevented him from smashing his head against the coffee table. But in the long run, his life could not be saved. He was hospitalized for months, partially paralyzed. She visited him every day, trying to cheer him up and give him some relief from the daily routine of the hospital. But eventually, his physical resources gave out, and he died.

Ann was distraught, but she collected herself, closed out her life in New York, and returned to Chicago. While she was recovering from her yearlong trauma, she was cared for by her family, including a cousin who was a doctor and an uncle who brought her chocolate milkshakes nightly.

It was winter in Chicago—cold, windy, dark early, void of things that would interest a woman whose husband had recently died.

Then Ann got unexpected news about Forrest. A relative called her and said "I have something to tell you about Forrest Ingram." Ann began to cry. She said: "You had better not tell me anything bad about him. I couldn't take it." "No," said the relative. "It's not bad news. Annie, Forrest is getting divorced." Ann's tears stopped immediately and the water from her eyes climbed back up her cheeks. She convulsed, but a smile spread across her face. She thanked her relative profusely.

After she collected herself, she called to the law office where Forrest worked as an attorney. She left a message for him to call her. But he did not call back.

During the week, a call came to her from someone with an unfamiliar name. She did not recognize the name and so did not accept the call.

After a week had passed, a strong determination grew in her. She was sure something was wrong. She again called the law office. She told the receptionist that she had left a message for Forrest but he had not called back. She said: "He must not have gotten the message, because the Forrest Ingram I know would have called me back immediately."

Shortly thereafter, Forrest called her. The confusion was cleared up: the first message for Forrest had been put in another attorney's box; he was the one that had called her, but she did not recognize his name. But when Forrest got her message, his heart flip-flopped. He called her back right away.

They talked for a long time: she telling him about the death of her husband, he telling her about his pending divorce. Before they hung up, they had made arrangements to meet on January 30 for their first date. The liturgy of love was about to begin.

Love's Liturgical Cycle

This book celebrates events in the love life of Forrest and Ann Ingram. To them, each of the events is sacred, awe-inspiring, uplifting, profound. They hope true lovers will read these poems and be inspired by them to enjoy and revere their own love lives.

These poems focus on momentous events remembered yearly: the mystical birth of Ann, the magic of the lovers' seemingly ordinary first date, the heart-and-soul rocking experience of the first time they made love, and their eternal and formal commitment to one another in marriage. The volume also includes numerous love poems highlighting everyday rituals, like sharing a kiss when Forrest comes home from work.

The poems are gathered into groups, celebrating the cycle of the lovers' feast days, plus a special section for "ordinary time" expressions of love. Just as the Christian liturgical cycle begins with the birth of the central figure of Christianity, so too does this volume begin with the birth of the poet's muse, Ann, the central figure of all these love poems.

SUMMARY OF CONTENTS

I

BIRTHDAY OF A GODDESS

December 21

To Forrest, Ann's birthday is a real but mystical and mythical event. It happened in late December, like the birth of Christ. How could she not be his "goddess"? Indeed, she is "Like Venus" appearing on the half-shell, as depicted in the famous painting "The Birth of Venus," by Botticelli. His first contact with her is conceived as the "Ear Tickle" of a soft siren on the breeze. It was a "world-altering moment" when Ann appeared in his life ("Ready to Rule Me"), and he adored her daily ("Monotheism").

But Annie was also always for him a "Little Girl in the Sandbox" who nevertheless owned the universe from the moment she pushed her way into the world ("No Way"). He was enraptured by the rhythms of her dancer's body and by her cheeks, her alert eyes, her expressive eyebrows, her full-flowing hair ("FACE—The Music of It"). Read the poems.

Birthday Poems

Ear Tickle
Like Venus
Ready to Rule Me
Monotheism
Little Girl in the Sandbox
No Way
FACE—The Music of It
may be
A Birthday Card
That You Are
Above the Ground
Wear Me
Accentuate the Positive
Not Gold Nor Gilded Monuments
Like Loving

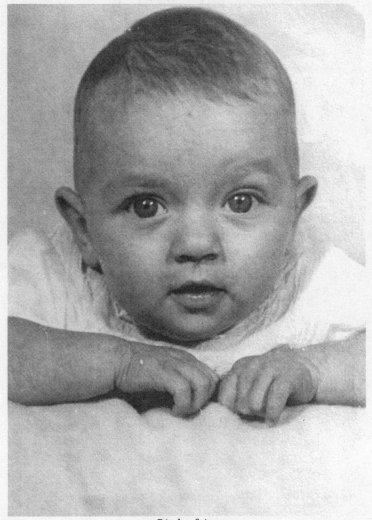

Birth of Ann

EAR TICKLE

I

I felt you first as a tickle in my ear
when I was a teen, green and troubled.

My parents were no doubt traveling,
visiting friends in a Chicago burb;
I was sitting up tense in the back seat,
suddenly, this sensation: a pleasing buzz
bothering my inner ear.

        You must have
whistled for me, (but no, how could
a toothless kid shape such sounds?
and how could you have known
I was anywhere near to send out such sounds?).
Still a soft siren, singing, you came to me, beloved,
on the breeze, bathing my face with music
through the open window.

        I sat up,
tense. Your melody like a magnet drew me out—
out of the window like a figure from Chagall
flying to his beloved, or a leaf riding the wind.
An eagle, I soared above the car, above the crowded streets
searching for--something, someone--I did not know.

Then the music diminished, like a promise
for not now. I folded my wings and alit again
in the suddenly stuffy car.

A memory
only, a music lingering like an after-aroma
of meadows and green things with flowers
throwing fragrances all over my body,
music I hearkened to at night on the edge
of sleep. You were in the atmosphere
like stars in the daylight, like a moon
rising on the other side of the earth,
coming, expectant, sure to arrive.

II

Then, there you were at my door, assessing
my feet flung up on my desk. You sighed out
that music, that bouquet of fragrances
I had ceased hoping to hear or smell.

Today, we celebrate but one birth, the day
we both were born. Time collapses in on itself.
Both of us are still but babies,
with fresh visions, untested tastes.

We cannot celebrate one being born
without the other.

Venus at the Beach

LIKE VENUS

Like Venus, you burst
Fully formed, onto life's stage
Ass, sass, all!

And chimerically came to me
Like a wounded beast
Howling love
Into lonely night.

Elemental, raw,
Metaphysical, refined,
You are all elements to me:

The *earthly* aromas
     of your creamy perfumed flesh;
The melodious tempests
     of your *airy* mellow tones;
The liquidity
     of your sensual movements over my eyes
     like *waterfalls* over old rocks;
And the consuming furnace of your *bonfire*
     embraces.

Luminous diamond!

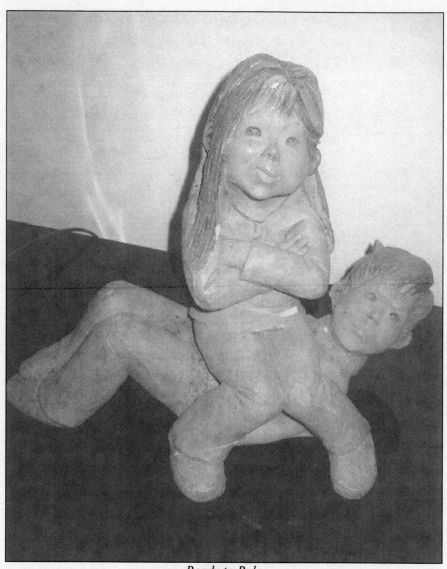

Ready to Rule

READY TO RULE ME

When she was born, she was already
ready to rule. She spat out her eddy
and took charge of the neighborhood,
organizing events as only she could,
beating the bottom of her sandbox pail,
raising her eyebrow, nibbling a nail
while deciding the fate of some hope-
less male admirer or other dumb mope.

When she entered my space, the gleam
in her bright green eyes revealed a dream
hidden behind them and awoke in me
a sense of encountering my destiny.

Used to being boss, I had to bow
and accept just how she would, from now
on, dominate my thoughts and rule
my desires. No, she was no fool
so she knew what to do and what to be
to bind me to her and to make of me
her lover, adorer, protector—her ONE,
her ONLY, as I have surely become—
willingly so, ecstatically so—
where in the world would I want to go?
Where to be, if not with her
who, being born, became, as it were
a sign in the sky, a word from on high,
that she was not only the apple of my eye
but the breath I breathe, the joy of my heart,
so that never ever could we be apart.

What a world-altering moment when this girl was born--
the night gave way to everlasting morn;
darkness departed and radiance grew--
it was all, it seems now, that ever I knew.
My babe in the sandbox, be with me I pray.
I love you forever--forever and a day!

MONOTHEISM

You must have butted your way into the world
Ass first, my fire-suffused goddess.

Like two suns rising, you dawned, setting aflame,
Unpurpling, crimsoning the cloudfields.

The groins of Olympians males--Ares, Hephaistos—
Burned. They began to vie that very day.

Ass-first, you fell from time's womb into my lake.
Once placid, my recesses were suddenly aboil.

My depths, in turmoil from your unquenchable heat.
My sands, ripped away, swirling desperately.

The impotent gods held back, amused, perhaps
Afraid of such a death. Jealous--and no doubt.

I lunged at your heart and wrestled you
With blistered hands and charred emotions.

In my lake, you sizzled, sent out rhythmic signals.
I smothered you with adoration; you me with hot love.

We die together every day we live, eternally.
Under my waves, you glow gloriously forever.

Your flame dances for me only. Let Aphrodite scowl.
For me, there is one goddess only.

Ann on Top

Little Girl in the Sandbox

That's my Annie over there, my little girl,
See, over there, that devilish curl
Hanging in the middle of her forehead
Just above her flashing eyes?

She never brushes it away, it stays
There, bouncing back and forth, as if to say:
"This is my realm, this huge sand box,
This earth, where I am queen."

                    The sand
Is hers, the pail, the shovel, the day,
The night, the sea, stars, air,
Water, height, weight, wisdom,
Knowledge, goodness, all. All hers.

So, it is her birthday. So, what can I give?

I have nothing that is not hers. Nothing. I live
For her, all year, day in and day out.
That's what my life on this earth is about.

So, Annie, hey, Annie!
                    Over here!

You are my one and only, my dear,
Dear everything. I give you: my life,
This little gift, only this, my little life.

NO WAY

I am grateful
for that fateful
      day.

You crawled down the tunnel
And stuck out your head,
Looked around and said
(or were about to say)
      "No way!"

You were about to turn,
And crawl back in
But then some dern
Power from behind
Pushed you and out
      You fell.

Into the harsh world.
Into a world of possibility.

In no time,
(thank heaven!)
With a little swagger
And swing of ass
And a raised eyebrow
(Quizzical and demanding)
You tamed the universe.

And me.

FACE--The Music of It

There is a music in her face.

I hear it when her half-closed eyes
Croon dreamy love songs to me
As we lie abed.

And there above the subtle
Expressions of one green orb,
Her left eyebrow, musing,
Unleashes a quiet cadenza
Of pastoral flute flights,
Or questioning, summons an oboe-note
Long-held and high above all other sounds.

Her pomegranate cheeks when she smiles
Or laughs outright at my mild jokes,
March forward like a band of blazing coronets
Piercing my soul's ear and making me
Twirl my previously placid baton.

Her lips, relaxed into a demur smile,
Even without speaking, let loose
Cello resonances from Bach suites.
As she shapes words, complimentary strings
Swell fortissimo or diminish pianissimo
From her upper and lower lip.

And oh, how her viola voice
Wraps me round
With subtle innuendoes
As we sip our "toons"
On an evening after work!

Her wave-like hair cascades
Like swirling waters in a singing brook,
Then rushes in dancing rhythms
Down around her cheeks
In a flourish of French horn ringlets.

I cannot but believe that God
Created music with her in mind,
And her with me, and I with her.

He gave audio to my eyes
To hear the melody of her beauty.
I perceive the symphonies and songs
That she so effortlessly creates
With every change of expression.

All the shapes of her visage are alive
With the divine sound of heavenly music.

Why does God today bless *me*
With such a gift? After all,
It's *her* birthday!

may be

every day is your birthday

(may be)

when the tiny passageway of possibility
that sometimes binds your brain and heart
into a bundle of anxious expectation

can be tickled open

cajoled or compelled

(may be)

to reformulate and lubricate itself

into a carefree breathtaking lighthearted waterslide

to deliver you lickety-split

into the wide

free

world

now

our world

(may be)

A BIRTHDAY CARD

It seems so awfully simple
To offer you my dimple.

Your fingers fondle my tresses
With loving luscious caresses.

Along your spine, a ripple,
As my fingers explore your nipple.

Our lives and juices blend;
Our love shall never end.

THAT YOU ARE

I am secretly in love with
you.

When *frothing at* the mouth
and being a complete louth

it's because I **NEED** you
and can't stand things that get in the way like

sleep, exhaustion, work, bills, tensions, **me**
in love with you.

I hope you understand--
the absence of you makes my heart

go **MAD**

in love with you

secretly

I go **around** in the big world
but what do I **see**
(nothing, really)

I watch **you**
I study the expression on your face

Meanwhile you chat on, you cook,
you exercise, you plan and make wonderful
arrangements of our lives together while i

secretly, still

worship you in the **anguish** of my heart
when I am not with you
or, with you, not actually with you but hoping

THAT YOU ARE!
because it's EVERYTHING
to me, your secret admirer

Forrest L. Ingram | 19

ABOVE THE GROUND

I know how your feet
dance above the ground when you walk

how you throb in my mind
when you stand in the kitchen making dinner

how your fingers excite my fancy
when you cut a red pepper

how your eyes make my heart explode
when you look up from Bon Appétit

I feel how your little finger
adjusts my temperament, my day

how your leg over mine at night
is stronger surety than castle walls

how lying beside you on the beach
shoos away anxiety, relaxes me utterly

how dancing with you transports me
into an Eden of you and me

WEAR ME

I sing the sudden surprise of your ringlets
bouncing like banshees over your brow
the fabulous form of your flawless face
cherryapple cheeks under cha-cha eyes
a double of dimples never outdone
felling fawners who seek your favors
but, frowning, you deflate and flatten them
forever but me alone you favor always
with fondness and finest feelings

the beauty of your breasts nobody can gainsay
your shapeliness simply sings its own song
so heavenly earthly, who hears it not?
your music maddens all males who are near

a bauble in a box, a broach on a chain
are acts of another to which we accede
these words are mine, for mine own mate
one, only, always, and ever: Ann, my Annie

my living words will wear wonderfully long
outliving all but the Everlasting Lord
they highlight the face far far fairer
(the oxbow eyebrow of arched amusement)
than silvery braids of burnished beads
they show more sexy the sensuous thigh
(the sizzling sinews of smooth muscle
and the arch of the sassiest ass in existence)
than the languishing flow of liquidy lace

all my wild words, wear, my love
wherever you will, however you wish
in buxom bosom bronzed by the sun
around your artfully sculpted arm
or fastened to finger finer than a jewel

belted at your belly, bright like a star
a spark on your ear, on your hair a spangle
atop your shoe a perched diamond, silk
smooth on your skin, in your heart a hunger.

wherever you are, wear my words
my love, wear me.

At Dinner

ACCENTUATE THE POSITIVE

If you're ever feeling low
And the world seems blue
And a sea of swirling shit
Starts to cover you.

Keep your head above the muck
And walk in promising sunlight
Rejoice in your singing veins
Take refuge in delight.

This month, the death of the year,
We celebrate your birth
The day you dressed in the raw
And boarded planet Earth.

We can't just party nonstop
Each December day
But we can count our blessings
And that may make us gay.

Oh, the darling of my life,
Applecheeks Butterfly Ann.
Never so fine and fiery a wife
Has ever had any a man.

NOT GOLD NOR GILDED MONUMENTS

gold I give you, gold girl, (not),
emeralds, my emerald-eyed love
to make shimmer the sun's sheen
or dance elfin-airy near your eyes

(neither) (nor) (not this time)

diamonds in a diadem decorating your brow
(no) rubies rich rose red
(can't) seven sensuous sapphires or
opulent opaque opals ('fraid not)

but wondrous: words, word, words
wheel out of me, whir like a wagging world
of tongues to tattle on your "tendernesse"
brag of your bold beauty, and most
give grateful gratitude to God.

LIKE LOVING

Like a willow
Rhythmically swaying,
Moved by mystic winds

Like a beach ball
Bouncing among laughing children
At the edge of the immense sea

Like aromatic cuisine,
Surrounded by sensuous scents—
My juices all a-jumble.

Like the red-orange sun
Hovering at the horizon over our January lake,
Light sparking off melting ice.

Like so many things somehow
Spare, strange, magnetic
Unique, catching the eye, the ear

Like
Song of water rushing over rocks
A single swallow swooping into a tree
Or a flock of gulls landing on the beach

Like
Hot tangerine embers bursting against flagstones
Mozart's signature flourish to end a phrase
The shimmering ecstasy of "Starry Night"

Like
Kentucky pasturelands with thoroughbreds prancing
A confusion of wildflowers huddled against a mountain
And each memorable satisfying moment of every day

Yes,
Whatever excites the senses and awakens the mind
Reminds me how much I like
Loving you.

Ann by a Tree

II

FUN DAY

Love can be light-hearted, expecting that there will be many good times to share. At the same time, when lovers first meet, they may not believe immediately that they have found the one they were intended to be with always. They test one another. They put a wet finger up to see which way the wind is blowing.

On January 30, Forrest rang Ann's bell. She opened the door. He held in his hands two gifts, a book and a bottle of wine. The book was *Bluebeard*, by Kurt Vonnegut. It was about a man and a woman who met and fell in love. The wine was Beaujoulais Villages, a fresh new vintage with a sparkling taste ("Yesterday").

They talked for a while, then decided to share a drink. Ann reached up to get the Scotch glasses on the top shelf. She stood on her tiptoes. Forrest watched, thrilled ("And That Was It"). Before long, twenty years had passed and they knew that, even though they had "fenced/Like warriors" and fought like puppies, ("Tomorrow Is"), electrifying love dominated their lives and they yearned for another twenty years. Read the poems.

Fun Day Poems

And That Was It
Yesterday, Our First Fun Day (Song)
Entering Eden (Verses for "Yesterday")
Fun Possibility
I and U
Made for One Another
Fun Knows
Fun Day Thirteen
About Love
Fun Forever
Seventeen
Monday Funday (A Ditty)
Adult Love
Tomorrow Is (Another Twenty Years)
20 (More)
Let's See: A Vision

That Was It

And That Was It

A month before you first unzipped your skirt
for me, we sat demurely round
the round white table, quite alone.

You wore those sensuous thin
tapering legs you never take off
atop high heels.

You offered Scotch, I said yes.
You reached for glasses, top shelf,
and that was it.

Your skirt slid up your leg
where my hand should have been
and that was it.

Your sweater clung to your breasts
your perfect ass cried out my name
and that was it.

We confessed how we had longed
always for one another, but could not,
would not cross the line.

Nonchalantly on edge, we sipped
and drank each other in. We let imagination
fill the blanks.

You were healing from a husband's death,
I completing a contentious divorce.
The time was ripe.

Saliva mingled with our Scotch; the fragrance
of serious banter engulfed us. Gently, a Power
pushed us together.

We gathered coats to face January's chill.
I offered a road map for all our years.
You smiled a Mona Lisa smile.

"Let's see if we have fun," I said.
And that was it.

Yesterday, Our First Fun Day
(A song)

Yesterday,

It was like yesterday,

You opened wide the door

And took from me

These paltry gifts

The book, the wine

I bore.

Yesterday,

It was our first fun day,

You opened wide the door

And took from me

These precious gifts

The book, the wine, my HEART

I bore.

ENTERING EDEN
(Recitative for "Yesterday")

On the eve that our new-born love began
To live, you saw on your porch a man
Bearded with a bottle of Beaujolais
Crooked in his arm in a jaunty way;
In the other hand like urgent mail
A modern resurrection tale.

Refrain: Yesterday...

How long did we pause upon the porch?
Your eyes were ablaze as if a torch
Were lighting you, goddess, to your throne--
My heart! January can freeze the bone.
That night, a bonfire consumed my heart--
What a wonderworld was about to start?

Refrain: Yesterday...

Your smile broke over me; you opened the door
I crossed the threshold. I know no more
What we said, how you took the book,
Bluebeard, or when my heart first shook
With hope you were the one, the only,
And I would nevermore be lonely!

Refrain: Yesterday...

To what heady heights you lifted me
With your leather skirt above your knee.
Your upraised arms pulled your sweater tight
And your breathtaking breasts blinded the light.

Your flesh felt my eyes rove toe to head
Up calves, round ass; my fears all fled.

Refrain: Yesterday...

It was our first day in Eden. We sat and talked
Over our scotch; neither of us balked
At telling our woes, our hopes, our dreams.
We would walk the world, wade in the streams,
Hike the woodlands, hear concerts, see plays,
Grateful that our hours would grow into days.

Refrain: Yesterday . . .

After this encounter, it was impossible to conceive
Ever leaving my woman. Could Adam leave Eve?
We were given this world; we were given our time --
Surely to enjoy it could be no crime.
Marvell and his mistress made the sun run;
So we sang like children: "Let's see if we have fun!"

Refrain: Yesterday. . .

Fun Possibility

I

Buffeted by psychological storms,
              By pain
You yet endured, while insanely
The vengeful one held her silence
              Like a gun.

She laced your childhood with real fears,
              Abused you
With chimeric promises that disappeared
With each new day, replaced by moral
              Hypocrisy.

Disappointment in your father haunted you
              Daily--
His dread, his sad state, his refusal
To stand, to live. You call into his tomb:
              Lazarus, come.

You got tangled in wrong turns, twists
              Of fate,
Choices gone awry, marriages, mismatches.
You sought safe times with elderly dicks--
              Wealthy charmers.

Underneath the world's swirl and burly,
              Your soul
Sought some haven from running,
From abuse and disappointment,
              Some peace.

II

The past lives in dreams, in memory,
    In the brain,
In the skin, in muscles tightening,
In pain. It never dies forever as long
        As life pulses.

Had you not been tossed enough by life,
        Odysseuslike?
Your ship passed mine one day on open sea.
Our hearts jumped, we waved, but our bodies
        Sailed on.

You landed in New York, another isle,
        For torture.
Exquisite--a noble husband, new-wed,
Exploded in your arms. Your nursed him lovingly,
        In vain.

In time, our ships docked together in
        Shared distress:
Your new widowhood, my imminent divorce.
I offered you *Bluebeard* and Beaujolais.
        We held

To one another for life, dear life. Would we
        Have fun?
When you reached for the Scotch, your breasts
Lifted my sagging hopes. You flashed
        A winning smile

Under liquid eyes. Before you faced me,
        Already
I had read every curve--calves and thighs
Diminutive waist, bulbous breasts, and
        Oh! luscious ass.

III

Our pleasures needed no cure, no balm,
        No other magic
Than themselves, ourselves. But your pains
Continued, enhanced by madness and mayhem
        I brought you.

To the curses of Lincolnwood, my dearest,
        My love,
I introduced the curses of Highland Park
On blackest nights when bats reigned
        They married

And generated ghouls to confound
        Our belfries.
But our communal monsters began to fade,
Their power drained by thought but most
        By love.

Through swamps we sloshed to firm green ground
        Where we
Might be, for good, ourselves and free
And sing each year, loud as can be
        "Let's see!"

I and U

You caught my "I"

When, gorgeously contoured in cashmire,

"U" reached high for the Scotch.

Ur nipples pressed tautly outward, and
The possibility of pleasures unending
Rippled down your form,
Arms, breasts, thigh, ass, calves.

U glanced over Ur shoulder and

Trapped my ♡.

I knew from the start that "I"

Had to have "U".

My "I" found its proper place

In Ur "U",

And learned to sing
New erotic songs in several tongues,
Lilting laughing tunes, sensuous aires,
Naughty rhumbas and salacious sonatas.
My bow on your strings makes shivering melodies.

I ♡ U always.

FUN KNOWS

Fun knows no holiday in our home.

Fun knows no one-day
Anniversary either.

Like the sun that never sleeps
It comes up through dark night,
Shimmers at the edge of mystery
Then climbs

Into clouds
To lurk in our libidos
Alert to the least clearing
A hole to dart through.

Or bursts with brilliance across our kingdom's lake waters
Revealing limitless all-blue horizons stretching forever.

It glints in your eye, in mine.
Suddenly our mouths must kiss,
Eat, suck; our tongues must explore,
Taste, lick; arms and legs must wrap
Around, squeeze; hands must press,
Slap; fingers pinch and scratch, unbutton;
Legs transport our bodies to bed.

Then
Calls your universe to mine and mine to thine,
Sensuous planets transversing endless space,
Yin to yang and yang to yin, with infallible radar
Finding one another and knowing: This is the one
Made for me before sun ever rose on any lovers
When God strewed upon blackness an infinity of seeds
And roared, though no ear was there to hear:
"Let's see if they have fun!"

FUN DAY THIRTEEN

Tumbling into love at first sight of you--

How not?-- our bones and blood

Imagined into being by divine playfulness.

Reaching for the tumblers--that did me in

Thirteen "see if we have fun" years ago.

Every evening, now, these limbs and hearts

Entwine; every dawn we are one rose opening.

Newly, we sing each day that

Yesterday you opened wide the door.

Eons speed by, my heart and gaze

Arrested by your beauty--shape, sexy smile

Rare as a full rainbow on the lake; colorful, complete, and

Silly like pups, we go on tumbling, tumbling.

ABOUT LOVE

A Sonnet

About love, the masters rarely err:

They sing of raging storms disturbing the deep

Reservoirs of lovers' love who brave steep

Precipices to kiss. Such fiery feelings stir

A colony of scissor tongues and propagate a whir

Of evil Iagos. In agony, true lovers weep

For imperfection, for pain at parting. Sleep

Wakes fears their passions are mere gossamer.

But Love, when I see you, dark anxious night

Breaks into promising day. In our private bower

The cynics' tongues are dumb to terrorize

Our knowing flesh. Armed with *amour,* we fight

To find alone that God-blessed perfect hour

Where worry dies and fun new fills our lives.

Fun Forever

What fun can we carry between us

Like a wreath of redcheeked roses

Once I have crossed the fabled

Border of the Land of Decline

While you, my everblossoming beloved,

Tarry in the Kingdom of Evolving

Energy, your life a sprightly dance

Next to my leaden lope?

I long

To dance with you eternally,

Lifting your light and lithe

Music-absorbent little frame

And twirling, twirling till

Last lights fade and the sun

Sits on the brink westward

To rise again

And again.

Legs

SEVENTEEN

Seventeen,

You seemed but seventeen

When you opened wide the door

And gave to me

Such precious gifts:

The face, the form

I love.

Seventeen,

It's been now seventeen

The years since first we loved.

Throughout those years

You keep giving me

The face, the form, the heart

I love.

MONDAY FUNDAY
(A Ditty)

When you're planning for a Fun Day,
Do you schedule it for Monday?

No, you may set it on a Saturday
When work can wait while you go play,

Or plan to celebrate it all day one day
Rising late and cavorting on Sunday.

But if "Let's See If We Have Fun" day
Circumstantially falls on Monday,

Shout hallelujah, c'mon have fun, Babe,
And chase the blues from this Monday FunDay.

ADULT LOVE

I guess we have to grow up!
No longer can we say "it's just pup-
py love", no longer can we act
like a Peke barking at a cat
or a Siamese hissing at
a dirty dog. Where're we at, Cat?

We no longer can say we are teens
(emotionally betwixt-and-betweens)
since the lived love that's plainly seen
on our foreheads is surely plenty
more than immature thirteen
or even sweet but out-of-joint sixteen.

No, the clock instructs us aplenty:
we have been dating now full twenty
magical, mysterious, boisterous years,
highlighted by hilarity, tormented with tears,
safe in togetherness, yet wrung with wild fears,
and wanting no one else.

Despite all these reflections, I guess,
we cannot simply wish away the mess-
iness of erupting emotion. You will kiss
me madly, chew my cheek, hiss
in my ear, tonguing my dimple, and I
will swallow you whole, crush you, eye
your ass salaciously; then off go
the clothes, strewn around in no
particular order, like a hurricane hit
while we tussled in bed. Isn't it
inevitable? Try as may, we can
not rise to be "woman" and "man".

No matter how many years may pass,
because of the firmness of your ass,
and the hurly-burly and whoop and whirl
of the mad love of a "boy" and a "girl",
(and the tightness of your puss), we stay
youngishly longing, madly in love. May
we always be green and teen as we are today!

Delos

TOMORROW IS
(ANOTHER TWENTY YEARS)

Oh,

I know

We laughed a lot
And danced
And, like puppies, fought,
And fenced
Like warriors, and hiked
Up peaks
Through parks, and biked
Round lakes

But: Oh!

Did we have fun?

And

What about tomorrow?
Will there be pleasure
Or sorrow?

Oh,

I know

We've dined at fine
Places,
Our faces
Flushed, our bellies
Filled, ignoring the bill.

We've walked uphill
And down
In San Francisco town
In Napa,
Tasmania, Ketchikan where
We stared
At current-cresting trout.

We've harkened
To seals barking
Along Oregon's coast
And breasted the wilderness
Trudging for miles
On Vancouver isle
To bathe in Nature's pool
Like fools.

And, Oh!

We have smiled at a llama
Herding sheep
In steep Tennessee.
We have hiked the Smokies.
Sympathized with Oakies
In Steinbeck's Grapes of Wrath,
And marveled
As Anna's life unraveled
Word by word
In Tolstoy's masterwork.

But,

Really

Did we have fun?

OK,

It's true

We have broken open
The roof with angry yells
Like demons in hell,
And we have disturbed our neighbors
As we tore our flesh
Sighing and crying out loud
In sheer delight.
No one overhearing could tell
Whether we were in heaven
Or in hell.

But,

Say,

What do our picture-albums tell?

Our calendars? Well?

Countries we conquered,
Oceans traversed,
Life shared
Everywhere!

But did we have fun
These first twenty years?
Really?

And what about tomorrow?

Well,

Let's see.

20 (More)

1 x 20 and 20 x 1

Let's just see if we'll have fun.

20 x 1 and 1 x 20

Another twenty? That may be plenty!

4 x 5 and 5 x 4

But we're not greedy. Who's keeping score?

5 x 4 and 4 x 5

Thank the Good Lord—we're still alive!

10 x 2 and 2 x 10

We've nothing to lose, and our lives to win.

2 x 10 and 10 x 2

You love me still, and I love you.

LET'S SEE: A VISION

I

In seventeen hundred and seventy-six
A group of guys, a paltry mix
Met in a Pennsylvanian hall
To set a course that would encompass all---

All the dreams they would ever know
All the gardens they would ever grow
All the heart they would have to offer
All the happiness they had to hope for

All the life their country contained
All the sunny days, all the rain
All tensions they'd feel, and all the ease,
All wars they might fight, all eras of peace.

They sat 'round a table, a nation-to-be,
Envisioning new life, prosperity,
Energetic enterprise, fair treatment of all,
Hard work followed by having a ball.

Decisions were writ down, a start was made,
A declaration of the future condensed on one page
Aloud they shouted for proud "liberty,"
Their mood was hopeful but humble: "Let's see!"

II

In nineteen hundred and eighty-eight,
A man and a woman met for a date
They sat at her table and pondered a drink
(She was so gorgeous he could hardly think.)

He noticed immediately her feminine form
And reflected thoughtfully as she lifted her arm
To retrieve the Scotch and a tumbler glass
From a high shelf. (Yes, he took in her ass.)

He weighed the discovery. He wanted to hold her.
Then, coy, she smiled at him over her shoulder
The light in her eyes, the curve of her lip
Skirt above knees, hand on her hip

All shouted at him that the day had dawned,
That time and occasion had joined to spawn
An era distinguishable from all past times--
A moment that could flower into rhythms and rhymes.

Suddenly, poetry engulfed his soul;
He opened his heart to devour life whole.
They sipped their scotch, spoke of that and this,
(Wondering what might happen if they ventured a kiss).

Under her smile and debonair air,
Her mind and heart examined the rare
Moment when, after years as a student,
She wondered whether he would or he wouldn't

Transform from being her literature prof
To her lover, a companion to make her laugh
And enjoy the sunset and the stars at night,
Who would take care of her needs and treat her right.

On both of their faces there settled a dream
And in their eyes one could detect a beam
That probed the future for some sure sign
That their two lives were meant to entwine.

They thought of the joy their lives might contain;
They imagined the sunny days, imagined the rain.
They knew there'd be tensions and that tensions would ease,
And any wars they might fight would be followed by peace.

They sat at the table, their inner eyes opening,
Envisioning new life and humbly hoping
For gardens to cultivate, good times to share,
And all the happiness that their hope could dare.

But first the first step each had to take—
What kind of pronouncement should each of them make?
They looked at each other, laughed, and agreed:
Would they have fun? They said: "Let's see!"

Destiny Met

III

OH, ANN! DAY

February 27

When lovers make love, they express physically the intensity of their deep feelings toward one another. One cannot celebrate the love between a man and a woman and ignore sexual play, the tension of the crescendoing explosiveness, and the thrill and excitement of orgasm. The first physical expression of love often feels as if it takes place in a green wood ("Green and Golden"), in a lover's bower surrounded by wood nymphs ("Hallelujah!") or in an Eden where only the two lovers can hear the explosions of pleasure ("Oh, Ann!"). Or lovers may feel they are in a trance ("Dreamgirl"). But if they are lucky, the pleasures of physical love will last a lifetime ("Still Plowing"). Read the poems.

Oh, Ann! Day Poems

HALLELUJAH!

Oh, Ann!

Dreamgirl

Evermore

Sixty-Five But O!

Green and Golden

Tongue Tied Up

Still Plowing

Oh!

Oh, Ann! 2011

Hallelujah!

HALLELUJAH!

I awoke amazed in a muddled wood
To a distant clarion call--a name
Sounding in my fevered brain
And on my lips.

My passion pursued the clear note's echo
Down a tangled path, through briars and brambles,
To a door in the hedge that was walled about
In the Wood of Lincoln.

Her bright eye searched me through the peephole; the door
Fell away. Her hand suddenly in mine
Pressed on me the key to Bliss's Bower;
Our bare feet rode there on rose petals.

Dryads, naiads, druids, nymphs
Sang with full throat from trees,
Rivulets, caves, and flowers,
Crescendoing to a hallelujah chorus.

We found a bed in a little green house
Built by fairies for our flesh to meet
One another in a first feverish embrace.
As I gazed into her flushed face, I cried:

Oh, Ann! My Ann! My always Annie!
Oh, Ann!

OH, ANN!

You make the dying sun
Linger in a fire-drenched sky
To contemplate your arched foot
Toe-ing the sand.

Your tongue turns tiny sauced tails
Of marine decapod crustaceans
Into omens of the heaven I feel
When yours probes the underside of mine.

You make the treble pling
Of Winston's Bachean meditations
The trembling of angel's lyres
And our souls' stirring volcanoes.

Your emerald eyes, that smile
You stole from Aphrodite,
Turns any day, any time or place
Into Paradise.

In love, I find the power lost
By Adam and Eve when error and evil
Made them vagabonds. When I insert
My key, Eden lives, the garden regained.

I love you with a missionary's love
I love you as a cowboy rides his hoss
I love to examine you, quite professionally,
I lose my mind in your tumultuous scents.

OH, ANN! stars blaze across the skies.
OH, ANN! lava pours from my eyes.
OH, ANN! I push against the garden gate.
OH, ANN! OH, ANN! my destiny, my fate.

DREAMGIRL

I

I had a dream the other night, O man!
About a gorgeous girl whose name was Ann.

Her lips were luscious and her breasts were grand,
Her legs the shapeliest in all the land!

Up she reached to grab a glass for me,
Up went her leather skirt above her knee.

She poured the scotch; we joked and laughed a bit;
Her rosy cheeks were warmer than my wit.

II

That dream-scene faded, and a green house grew
In an enchanted wood, where a brook ran through.

We wined and dined to a wood-nymph's song
About love that would guide us to loving ere long.

Hymen, it seemed, gave his nymphs command;
We kissed, we winked, we took each other's hand.

I led my love into my makeshift bower.
Our bloods were pulsing; I felt the power.

III

What happened next, I struggle to know—
The scene, of a sudden, melted like snow.

Light filled the bedroom where I lay in a daze;
Then her kittenish smile emerged through the haze.

"Was" is a memory, recalled in a dream,
"Is" is reality, even better than "seem."

She fingered my loin and played with my nip,
Cradled my head and kissed my lip.

So I drew her to me, and as long as I can,
I will hallow this day with a soul-filled: "Oh, Ann!"

Dreamgirl

EVERMORE

Fourteen years ago a leather door
Lifted (like fog lifts off the meadow floor
When intense sunlight kisses the moor).
I swallowed your eager eyes, ate the core
Of you (as if devouring from a sweets store
A wizard's confection). What I bore
In trembling arms was undoubtedly more
Than my arms had ever clutched before.
We left behind the jungle, wars, the lore
Of trolls, and found ourselves on a shore
Where new waves washed us. "Evermore"
Echoed in our flesh. It was no chore
To finger the lock, insert the key, and roar:
        "Oh, Ann!"

We have wandered a year in metaphor,
Pilgrims searching for our souls, floored
A twelve-month past when a doctor tore
Our guts out. "Nothing" was the score
He promised us. We fled to explore
Eastern alternatives, Chinese lore
Pills of deception from an exotic store.
Exhausted, we could no longer ignore
That salvation lay on a Western shore.
In went the scalpel, out poured the gore;
But there were you with: "You, I adore"
Now white waves wash us. "Evermore"
Echoes anew in our flesh. No chore
To finger your lock, insert my key, and roar:
        "Oh, Ann!"

Sixty-Five But O!

When I see winter, all naked sticks and snow,

Mocking my threadbare head, and your springtime face

Radiating like a halo of flowers in a vase, then I know

You are running laps ahead of me in this human race.

When I see you prancing up a daunting hill

And dancing on the mesa atop it, then I dream

Of capturing you, my prey; drawn by that thrill

I plunge reckless up after you, at full steam.

Laughing like a schoolkid first discovering fun,

Then carrying the knowledge with him as a man,

I relive catching you. When day is done,

I mount you, howl, shiver, shout: "Oh, Ann!"

(An appropriate rhyme for the word "alive"

Is a number I once feared: "sixty-five.")

Gift-wrapped Girl

Green and Golden

In a green world, I found you, Oh, Ann!
Lying on a bed of fragrant flowers.
I stared into your eyes, not believing
Not daring to, but seeing your cheeks
Suffused, the light of delight
In your emerald eyes, I knew

Oh, Ann! You-- You are the one.

We fucked green that day, my dick
Tauter than any twig of newborn sapling,
Your fingers teasing my tense trunk.
I trembled like an aspen all a-titter.

In our house of green, when our love
Was sprouting, we leaned longingly
Into one another, panting, our teeth
Floating like logs at a waterfall,
Our souls like leaves laden
With daylong drizzle in a rain forest.

Now in our golden world, Oh, Ann!
We fuck, though I grow brown with age
Your fresh-flower fingers enliven me
Your sinewy arms like vibrant ivy
Embrace my thick sap-filled trunk.

Not years ago, but now, Oh, Ann!
We drink in one another's souls
From deep inside our intense rapt gazes--
Our cheeks flushed, our mouths trembling,
We erupt, and laughter, like hot lava,
Rolls from our astonished mouths.

Oh, Ann! You-- You are the one.

Tongue Tied Up

What I have to say
On "Oh Ann!" Day
I say with tongue.

No breath of lung
But tongue alone.

No resonating tone
No tongue in cheek
No need to speak

Just round and round
Your sensory mound
That luscious O

Till you yell "Oh!"

STILL PLOWING

I

It's 20 years since first my stick
(More commonly appellated "dick")—
A lucky stiff, if I may say
And lustier than the month of May—
While languishing, lengthily lonely,
Came upon you, by invitation only,
(After years in which we both digressed
You in your waywardness, I in my mess,
Mapping wrong routes, missing right,
Moping and hoping in mid of the night)
And unashamedly by God's great grace
Being brought (at last now) face to face—
In a green house reminiscent of Eden
Not too long after supper was eaten
(Not an apple, mind you, but chicken, I think,
No devil peeked in to throw us a wink)—
Down your lane I came and through your gate,
My key in your lock, we unloosed our fate.
I gave it to you and you sucked me in
While God's face broke into a giddy grin.
We came together: woman and man,
And that's when I let out the cry: "Oh, Ann!"

II

From that day forward, we knew we were one,

Everything had changed, the moon and the sun,

People and places, the stars and the wind.

By the way we walk and talk, we send

One message writ large to everyone around:

"The earth we walk on is holy ground.

If you want to approach, this way it must be:

I AM FOR HER AND SHE IS FOR ME."

In our private field, you lay you bare

For me alone to plow you there.

The tingle and torment, the drawn out jolt

I feel as I turn you, explodes in a bolt

Of pleasure so intense I could almost say

The world was created for us today!

And we find as we till this sacred sod

That our plantation is inhabited by Umigod.

And my stick (it's clear to woman and man)

Plows one field only forever: "Oh, Ann!"

Oh!

I'm sure we both know
What made me say "Oh!
Ann!" that memorable night
When I, as your beau,
And you, too, were so
Filled with joy and delight!

We could have said "No,"
Or called up the po-
lice to break us apart,
But from head to toe
We were "in it," so
We gave one another our heart.

Oh, Ann! 2011

Gee, I'm glad to be your beau!
I love you, Wu, from head to toe—
your eyes, your cheeks, are all aglow,
Your shiny teeth, as bright as snow,
greet me when you smile.   The flow
of your luscious hair, not tied in a bow,
makes me cock my head and crow
with delight! Your strong-smooth shoul-
ders are a thrill to caress. Then, lo!
I feel your breast—oh! oh! oh!
I grab your ass, so firm and so
finger-tingling smooth. Then low-
er, front, I find the field I sow
my seed in when we have a go.
No Bill or Jerry, Jim or Joe,
no rich man, poor man, friend, or foe
will I let near you; they can all go
jump in the lake—it's no, sir, no!

You make me a king though I feel like a schmo;
you make me roar like Santa: Ho!
You make me remember or forget I know
what causes me pain, what causes woe.
You let me roam; you hold me in tow.
But you're all mine, dear, my Annie-o
from ankle to ear, from finger to toe,
your arms, your legs, I love you so!
What ever comes, how the wind may blow,
Every year, you're mine, my dear, dear: OH!
OH, OH, ANN!

IV

ANNIVERSARY

September 2

Lovers who know that they were meant to be together often make a public proclamation of their intention. We all know: it's called "getting married." When they marry, they profess to give one another their lives. ("My Gift"). At every marriage, there are skeptics that call enduring love "unreal" and say it will never last. But true lovers make the myth of a perfect union a reality ("4383" and "Endless Story"). As the years pass, married lovers celebrate their deepening love, year after confirming year. ("Eleven Stanzas for Eleven Years," "Sixteen Years, Sweet", "Eighteen", "Twenty Quick and Quirky Years,"). When love is total, time ceases to toll its bell and lovers feel that time simply ceases to exist. ("Yes, I Love Her").

Ann and Forrest were married on the anniversary of the marriage of Forrest's parents, Herschel and Vivian, who had been lovers all their lives. ("Not a Crowd"). Though they had raised seven children, they never lost the excitement, energy, and thrill of loving one another madly. When Herschel came home from work, he would pick up his wife Vivian and twirl her about, kissing her all the while. The celebration of enduring love is the subject of the Anniversary poems. Read them.

Anniversary Poems

My Gift
The Study of Inspiring Poetry
Sun, Rain, Lightning, Thunder
This Is Not a Poem
4383
Not a Crowd
Endless Story
Staying Home
Eleven (11) Stanzas for Eleven (11) Years
Jewels of the Heart
Sixteen Years, Sweet
Eighteen (If Only . . . Then . . . But . . . And)
Blessings Far and Near
Twenty Quick and Quirky Years
Twenty Little Things
Yes, I Love Her

Wedding

MY GIFT

What I give, you can't wear on your finger;

Only your heart.

What I offer won't fit in box or barrel;

Only your life.

Numbers, figures, words are ephemeral signs

Of actual gift.

Earth, concrete, emeralds, diamonds,

Just chemical solids.

Ink, words, documents, official stamps,

Merest intimations.

My dear, I give you nothing "real,"

Only my life,

Only my indestructible love.

The Study of Inspiring Poetry

Shall I compare thee to a Shakespeare sonnet?

Thou art more musical than his choruslines

Of tapdancing iambs with their twirling bonnets

Or pirouetting dactyls. Thy vaudeville shines

Brighter than his cleverest conceits.

No love scene has he penned that's hotter than

Thy sizzle in the stir-fry 'neath our sheets

Where, burning, thy beauty makes me most a man.

His perfect phrases are printed in men's minds

Less deeply than thy body on my soul.

Though every morn we part, my spirit finds

Thee always in me, and we two, one, are whole.

His readers rightly call his metaphors "fresh".

But I much prefer the poetry of thy flesh.

SUN, RAIN, LIGHTNING, THUNDER

Like the explosion of a red-hot sunrise

   the radiance of your smile!

Like a blazing furnace opened

suddenly,

into a wintry room

warming all

my secret places,

   the eruption of your dynamite kisses!

Like lightning over alpine peaks,

   the flashing of your magical eyes!

Like trembling rain clouds after thunder,

   my flesh when you are near!

THIS IS NOT A POEM

This is not a poem
you are

You are free verse dancing deliciously
over the pages of my heart

The gentle pressure of your legs
nightly on mine,
makes my soul
spread its wings and soar

Your hammer's rhythm on my obdurateness
cracks my defenses
my secret sealed spheres

The magnificence of your naturally cadenced forever beauty:
glaciers swinging slowly through mountain crevices
in the eternal sun whose refractions
dance with light feet on the silt-laden lake

You are volcanic upheavals
married to the frightened flight of a wounded doe

You are Mozart and Yanni enfleshed

my classic beauty

my hot Greek goddess

You are the poised perfection of an endless double-string

of priceless pearls

parading around the dark tan

of your sculptured neck

its tail wrapping gracefully

the wrist of your delicately contoured arm

No

not this is a poem

you are.

4383

I

Every day, it seems, the skeptics gain a fact,
Amass a hill of argument, a computer-full of numbers,
Statistical surveys, unassailable proofs,
Establishing anew, beyond a reasonable doubt,
Our love, like God, does not exist.

"Like God," they sing, wagging a knowing finger,
"The opiate-induced, chimeric delusional
Paste-up beast, child of chronic brain imbalances."

"Your unreal love," they chant; "has being only
On a silver screen, in a rose-colored world."

And if they concede us momentarily real,
Our fire, they prophesy, is doomed to cool,
Our loveboat bound to drift, then break against
The shoals of time, the hard cold rocks of life
And the sad story of Dorian Gray.

Our love, they opine, cannot withstand
The scummy news which creeps like worms,
Like baby dragons, from overturned stones.
They play hardball with us: they parade
Before us the orgies of the oval office,
The seamy affairs on Capitol Hill,
An endless cavalcade of aborted relationships,
Hollywood weddings, Reno divorces.

They produce sordid histories of once-fabled loves,
Decaying facades of royal unions undone,
Oceans of pumped up passion all gone dry,
Beached dreams, abandoned myths.

In short, they agree, we do not exist.

II

But we have our facts, love,
Our numbers, too, mount up
Against the skeptics. Numbers no one
Knows or could dispute. But we know.
Use abacus, fingers, high tech computer,
Lay these numbers end on end,
Encircling the globe,
Stretch them through the universe of stars,
Past Jupiter, past Venus, past far-distant Mars.

Here is a number to celebrate today,
A secret number for you and me:

> *Four thousand three hundred eighty-three.*

Whence comes this number? How is it told?
What is its meaning for you and for me?

> *Twelve times three sixty-five plus three.*

Twelve years since you and I first were wed
And as wedded lovers lay together in bed.
Add three days for February's curious habit
Of leaping once in four years, just like a rabbit.
   Three for divinity, three for the trinity,
   Four for the elements, eight for infinity.

Three sixty-five times twelve will yield
Forty three hundred eighty; then build
In the rabbity days and the total, you see,
Is *four thousand three hundred eighty-three.*

Four thousand three hundred eighty-three:
That number, as far as my soul can see,
Is divisible by nothing, it's as prime as can be,
Except one goes into it. Mathematicians agree,
It is one of a kind, a plural unique.

III

Old Greeks opined that the number, *four,*
Is the number of elements that make up our world:
Earth, air, fire, and water: our elements all,
Whether fucking or fighting or strolling the mall,
Listening to Mozart, humming a bar,
Or imbibing champagne with our tuna tartar.
Four are the corners of the rounded earth,
From which blow the winds of sadness or mirth
The trumpets' last sound, our death and new birth.

IV

Earth
Our passions perennially enfleshed
Our legs and hearts each night enmeshed.
Heaviness pulls us down into death
Despair makes difficult each labored breath.
We plant, we seed, we weed, we die
And with our bodies our hopes may lie.

Air
Our spiritual selves rise up in prayer
And God goes with us, everywhere.
We thrill to sensations of spiritual hue,
We walk arm in arm with each art's muse.

Fire
We bite, fight, lick one another's flesh, yell,
We turn back barely from the brink of hell,
We bury our noses in each other's smell,
We cling to one another, in the heat of the spell.

Water
We stroll in the misty cool of night
Hand in hand above anger and fright.
Anxiety flees as we dance in the rain
And sane ice chills our feverish brains.

V

Eight is two times elemental *four*
You-four, me-four; but there is more.
Turn eight on its side and what do you see?
The Mathematicians' symbol of infinity.

In the mind of God, before time began,
Before numbers troubled the mind of man,
When there was but One, and One was All,
You and I together heard God's one call:
Be, be together, be one, yes, be
From everlasting Now through Eternity.

VI

Three is the way the One appears to be
When turned toward humans. One He
Creator, the father whose love
Gave us us, and gave his son. One He
The son, who loved us through death,
Dispensed new life, and then, in a breath,
Poured out the Spirit, fresh wind, new fire,
Wakening us to our higher desires.

In *four thousand three hundred eighty-three*
Three flanks the single and the double we
So you and I and He and He and He
Are not five at all but mystically three
As He and He and He are One, too, and Three.
And the two threes, adding up to six,
Comprise two trinities--now there's a trick--
Father-Son-Spirit and God-you-me.
Four thousand three hundred eighty-three.

VII

Your head, my darling, the head I adore,
Must be dizzily swirling with numbers galore.

One: you are the one, the only,
Your head is one, your puss the only
One your ass, your mouth the only
Flesh I will drink from;
Your body, your form, a perfect unity,
Every part of you in exquisite harmony
Is one to my one, and we two are one.

Your head with two, I say two applecheeks
Each poised playfully under a flashing green eye
Above the dimples you sometimes deign to show
On either side of your classical nose
Above the striking chiseled chin
Beneath two ultra-sensuous lips
Concealing two rows of ivory teeth
Which nibble my nipple and bite my cheeks.
It hides as well that temptress tongue
You use to excite me from toe to thumb.

VIII

One next to two of course is twelve
As four plus eight and four times three
And twelve divides forty-eight by four
As three divides it by twice Mr. Eight.
Three plus three of course is six
And six into forty-eight is eight.
And eight on its side is everlasting,
The figure-skater's dream of mastery,
My dream of you goes on and on

As I contemplate your all-absorbing charm.
So the numbers say, as clear as can be:
I was made for you, and you for me

Four thousand three hundred eighty-three.

Washington, D.C.

4383

NOT A CROWD

Herschel and Vivian, and I and you
Were married together September 2

She was a woman with a spine of steel
He a man's man who yet could feel

I am not he
You are not she

Nor were we ever meant to be
Other than merely blessed we

Or as later we learned we blessed three
Like sailboat, sky, and vast blue sea

Each couple, I ween, thought a wee bit odd
One more old fashioned, one more mod

Each couple like peas in a two-pea pod
Pod and peas one in the mind of God

Like two leaves sprouting from one strong rod--
A dieffenbachia rooted in god-rich sod

We love but each other, eat alone, are odd
For two of us are three, yet but one UMIGOD.

Endless Story

We must have met in the garden before memory
Locked its gates on us and sent us east, out
From the perfect fruit trees and fragrant bowers
Where I bet we played together in those
Forgotten primal days before the great
Shutout darkened our senses and left us
Babes in unfamiliar and dangerous neighborhoods.

You--summoned, like Mary and Joseph--
Feared a man with a forbidding bearing,
A troubling name atop the Sullivan tower.
You paced, picturing the demanding ogre
Baring his wolf's teeth beneath bushy moustache.
He would lick his chops over your trembling grades.
Anxiety gripped you as you gravitated toward me.

There was something about the girl at my door
Peeking in, as I, my legs crossed at the ankles,
Feet resting on my desk, chatted on the phone.
I must have blushed, so you knew even then
There was some buried memory to release
From long bondage. I saw something—relief—
Flush the tension from your face. You sashayed in,
Confident now, bringing with you
The impression of perfect fruit and fragrant flowers,
I struggled to remember. Wasn't this woman
Someone I have known all my life?

You gave me some name I did not recognize;
I wanted to give you mine, to cover you
Forever. Your A's and F's intrigued me,
Your cheeks, your smile, the green light of your eyes,
Your siren breasts and tight-fitted taboo of an ass.
Weren't you someone I was destined to meet?

You bounced out of my office promising return,
Prancing away with a backward smile, tantalizingly
Thrown over your shoulder, and a book about traveling,
About "chataqua". You said you would come back.
But you never left. You were there again before time
Advanced—not an era passed, not a mythical moment.
We started, not knowing it, that day: our chataqua.

We wandered through books, conversations,
Up and down stairs, in and out of the chambers
Of our hearts. Our lives were tied
To tired pasts, too recent not to remember,
Not free, yet feverish to forge forward.

I was first to walk out of the picture; but
Something moved me to say: "I will
Always be here for you." Later, you called
And I came to your aid. You told family
In unrelated discourse, that "this guy" you knew,
Said this or that; compare, contrast.
Then you vanished behind wedlocked doors
In the tangled underbrush of New York.
I looked up from my books. You were gone.
Gone. The halls and stairwells were deserted.
Flowers stopped blooming, waters stood still.

We lugged our separate deserts with us, you
Through empty expanses, despite the crowds,
I parched and wilting in my arid prison here.
Where was your face, your swaying walk?
On separate paths we struggled up dunes
In our Saharan existences, hoping at each peak
To find one another. We found instead a sea
Still separated us, but touched both our shores.

I rowed a narrow path to a little green house,
A bower, a launching pad, safe haven.
I readied it—for what? For whom? All the while,
God at his workbench peddled the loom,

Picturing our paths together. He summoned you:
"Fly to another country, a distant shore nearby."
The earth shook when you, like Venus descending,
Set foot on the tarmac, crossed to the terminal
On dancer's legs, but with hurt heart brimming.

God cracked the great rocks, unchained the winds.
The gadabouts and gossips swirled out
"Ah," thought the writer, "what a story it would be!"
Buzz went the phones. And there you lay,
Almost lifeless. You heard my name and tears
Gushed down your cheeks. You heart heard
Disaster and doom.   But like the resonant song
Of whales in the dark deeps of wide waters,
You must have sensed an eternal call,
A whisper, an undertone, an incantation.
"You cannot tell me anything bad," you said.
She said, "He's separated, free." The tears rolled
Up your cheeks, faster than your erupting smile.

Life stirred in your veins again.
Dry-eyed you called; left your name.
But a cosmic joker confused the call-taker;
Who slipped the message into another's box.
So when he called--an unfamiliar name--
You waved it off. Agony stretched a week.
Out of your mind, you called again
Insistent, primal. Your call came to me
Like waves of music on a dark night
Under attentive stars. Our voices
Married right there, over the phone line.

And so we wed. The rest is: History--
Our History, Liturgy, Destiny,
Boundless Blessing:
                    Endless Story.

Staying Home

My first gift to you,

My love, today is

    Nine Two

    Ninety-Two.

I'm staying home

To play with you

    all day.

    What's say?

Cancel your plans--

You got your man

    With you.

    Yes, you do!

You know I am tru-

ly in love with you

    all ways,

    all days.

Eleven (11) Stanzas for
Eleven (11) Years

I

God is One; you were one (1) and I one (1) once.

II

The ones came two-gether (11), side by side.
As 7 comes 11, our two comes heaven

III

Faith, hope, love is Three; God is Three.
You, me, and God is also Three.
It takes the Three of us just to Be.

IV

Hand in hand, we climb the path
Winding up the rocky mountain
Facing sometimes daunting passes
Sometimes skipping through an open glade.

V

Called to life, yes, life, by the Creator
Who looked us over, said "This is good!"
Who set our feet upon this journey
Gave us light and dark, made us food
For one another, went with us on the way.

VI

Early on, the Lord of Living
Planted signs to guide our hearts:
A dimple deeper than the ocean
An apple cheek like bursting fruit
Cleansing laughter like adoration
Eyes, chin, legs, arms, heat, heart.

VII

Rounding a cliff we found our souls
Were face to face with an ancient rock
And, sitting atop, a shining figure
Who seemed to know us from long ago
Extended a thermos of living water
A sip of wine, a bite of bread
And a world to wake to if we went dead.

VIII

From his shoulder a snow-white dove
Swooped above us, flapping his wings
While water flowed and spirit and fire
Engulfed our hearts. Our eyes were opened
Like Adam and Eve when they first had sex,
But new. Our rocky path became our Eden
Your hand in mine, and the generous Three
Who gave me to you and you to me.

IX

Steeper and steeper the path winds round
Occasionally offering vistas of stunning colors.
We hear singing, we see mountain birds flitting
In and out among the dark cedars and firs.
We carry poetry in our hearts, drama in our gait,

Every step is a story, every word a song.
A guardian goes with us, invisible, discrete.
Up ahead is a grassy grove, shaded and secret,
We lie down and our flesh ad libs a symphony.

X

Sometimes as we climb, winds howl; snow and sleet
Beat down, and we cannot even find a place in the heart
For refuge. We climb into crevices and caves
Exhausted, embattled, bedraggled. Huddling
Against ancient enmity, the hatred of others,
In the dark, we lose ourselves, our vision, our hope.
We act like wild beasts, maniacs, an entire pack
Of snarling wolves, circling, snapping at one another.
We forget Eden. Oh, how black the world seems then
 From our dark cave! Death seems our only exit.

XI

Then, you touch my arm, I kiss your neck,
And we are ourselves again. A white butterfly plays
Among the flowers at our feet. Life bursts anew
From surrounding rocks, oozes from treetrunks
In the lonesome wood, wafts on the fragrances
Of mountain flowers, lilts in the warbler's song.
Eden comes back and our path seems less steep
Its slopes yielding more easily to our energetic steps.
We find a grove; fire races through our veins;
The guardian encloses us in a green tent,
God's smile is there too. And we are home.

Jewels of the Heart

The jewels I give you this day,
    My love,
Are not for show, not to wear
Proud on your delicate fingers,
    Your sensuous neck.

You live a rarer beauty; sparks
    Enliven
Your emerald eyes with soulfire
Where these spirit-gems may infuse
    White magic.

These jewels are in the mind and heart,
    In words,
My dearest, in Thomas Merton's living spirit,
Whom we met when we stood at his grave in
    Gethsemani.

These jewels are spirit; their luster
    Will not fade.
A saint's meditations have no value except
How you treasure them, how you wear them
    In your heart.

SIXTEEN YEARS, SWEET

1.
Just the other day, we started kissing
And couldn't stop until
The ceiling opened on the stars.

All day, all night, our bodies and our minds
Are wrapped together, entwined
In sleep, we send loud
Love messages through our bodies'
Passionate play, belting out bold arias.

2.
We are the owners of this suite,
My sweet.
You own me and I own you.

For all that you are and all that you do,
I hoard you, my love, no one but you.

3.
In our shared canoe, we paddle toward
The *terra firma* of a forever shore,
Calm, solitary, deep, firm,
Away from disturbing winds and minds.

4.
Fresher than any flower are you, my love
Hotter than sexy tango dancers.

You love me here, you love me there,
You give me joy in a world of wonders.

You are my today and my tomorrow
You are my now and my forever.

5.
Our fights are like nights cutting through a jungle
Searching for day and a meadow of peace.

Tigers and cougars crouch on branches
Awaiting the fell blow that leaves us both
Meat for their teeth.

6.
But you are my air, my fleshy sprite,
I live in you and you in me.

Luscious, voluptuous, juicy, and tight
And I--what luck!--hold you every night!

7.
Each day we wake to sunlight on the lake,
Gulls whirling over gentle blue waves.

When I am away, you are not deceived--
I am always here in your heart and mind.

More intimate than air, more durable than light,
My love surrounds you all day and all night.

Our kisses are blessings; God's blessings are kisses.
Wrapped in his kisses we know how to love.

I just want you to go around with just me
Everywhere, all the time, so everything can be real.

8.
You are my beloved in snuggles and caresses,
Laughing and weeping and sitting silent.

You are my beloved in tasting and wretching,
Dancing, strolling, playing, and being sad.

It's a pleasure to share with you Hecky's ribs
Ginger-curry cole slaw, laughter, and wine.

Always your touch brings me to life,
With your arms around me, living is all good.

9.
Mornings, I ache to press your flesh against me
And to admire your beauty from top to toe.

Your aromas are maddening, I can hardly stand it,
And your breaking smile sends a tickling signal:
You huff and you puff before gales of laughter
Spill on our sheets and make the walls tremble.

10.
Because of our love, intense and pure,
We can be free as God made us to be.

Every inch of your flesh is food for my heart
And my pulsing dick stiffens as my fingers play
Symphonies and love songs on your stretched out torso.

11.
At sixteen years, we are wild about each other,
My crazy cellmate, we belong in Dunning.

Crazy in love, but the knot is not
What binds us forever. No, it is not.

No, no. Nothing you can say or do
Can stop me from loving you madly forever.

My destiny from date of birth was loving you,
Your destiny and mine met in the stars.

What I love about you is simple to say:
Your eyes, your smile, your light caress,

Your warm weight against me, the way you stand,
Your arms, legs, your every breath.

I love you *now*; yesterday I loved you
Now; tomorrow I will love you *now*.

12.
Not years ago, but *now*, when we share
Our bodies, our teeth float out of our mouths,
We drink deep from one another's souls
And erupt, at last, in volcanic laughter.

Are we not still like teenagers? We love,
We fight, and (thankfully) we love again.

All of you was made for all of me.
The music of your movements, your dancer's poise,
Your fiery eyes, truthful soul, your genuine
Hearty laughter, a smile golden as sunrise,
Cherry cheeks, your fingers' caresses
Dominating my temples with delicate strokes.

What do I love about you, my one love?
Everything.

13.
Tears run down your cheeks into my soul
When you grieve, are anxious or overwhelmed.
I long to treasure up each tear between
My index finger and my thumb.

14.
In a million little acts, we say I love you:
Chopping, shopping, cooking, eating,
Sleeping, waking, touching, kissing,
Making coffee, making dinner,
Making out, making love.

15.
To where we should have been
God brings us round.
Life and love are simple when
You've found "The One,"
And there's only one One.

Each year we celebrate.
But we are still but teens,
Going backwards, its seems,
From January to September.
From 18 Fun Days to 16 for Wedding.
By such counting, I swear,
We'll never be adults!

16.
You are my muse, my amusing muse
No wonder poetry pours out of me!

Cruising Along

EIGHTEEN
(If Only . . . Then . . . But . . . And)

I

IF ONLY we had met when you were eighteen
Before the knot-tying, before your parade
Of Greeks and Serbs, before your flights
To Florida and New York, before the cold war
Morphed a parent and a child over tense times
Into standoff adversaries.

IF ONLY in 1968 on that October 18
You had blessed my birthday with your body
Dancing enticingly down P.C. Hooftstraat as I
Emerged from theological musings to catch
A glimmer of your sunny sashaying form
Lighting up the cloud-smothered Amsterdam street.

IF ONLY before I turned eighteen
I had had a vision of you, an apparition,
Holy grail in a grotto, or a shooting star.
Could I have resisted your fire, pulled over
My head the seminarian's black gown, tied
The tough cincture tight about my groin
And buried all thought of human love
In books and pure-hearted prayers, miles away
From lovelife reflections in moss-covered Grand Coteau?

IF ONLY we had suspected, somehow intuited,
When you were still a babe, the woman

You promised to become, sexy, compelling,
And we had understood, even then,
Though I was still an immature boy,
That we were made to be for one another
All to all, each other's sun and moon and stars.

IF ONLY you had popped out of the mirror
By the elevator in Roosevelt's Sullivan Tower
In the year '81 on tower-floor 18
And, wrapping me in your musical mystical power,
Had captured my imagination, and whisked me, willing,
Away, to be your man, your worshipper, forever.

IF ONLY I had sensed you somewhere
Behind the tree line, and had hunted you down,
Sniffing you out in the forest of desire
Before senselessly burying myself
For almost 18 years in a windowless cave
Where I dawdled, deadened, without knowing you,
Until you appeared miraculously at my cave door.

IF ONLY you had found the door to freedom
Out of your Lincolnwood prison, and had fled
To me before three other husbands temporarily
Laid claim to your flesh and Florida offered you
False solace and distracted you from finding me.
Or if Florida had offered you no solace at all,
So that, agitated and suspecting some other future,
You would have scanned the skies, and focused
Your alert mind and pounding heart to find me,
Finding no rest until you rested your head
On my chest, explored my chest with your fingers,
And felt my encircling arms protecting you
Like a steel shield.

II

THEN we would have embraced one another
From the beginning, fresh, virginal, pure
Of pasts, full only of promise. Our arms
And hearts would have carried in them
No troubled histories to unload or marginalize.
We would have had no trauma of divorce or spousal
Death to deal with; no murky madness with offspring—
No struggle with a pre-teen's painful resentments
No fateful bonding of your son to your mother.

THEN we might be celebrating eighteen
Years more than the eighteen during which
We have professed, and continue to profess
To the world: "This is my One and Only."

III

BUT would we then have been ourselves?
Who are we without our pasts? We cannot undo
Our histories. In God's wisdom, past events
Destined us to be, for one another, each:
The One and the Only.

IV

AND what a miracle that no disaster befell us
Even though at eighteen we could not meet
On a rainy narrow Amsterdam street.
Nor a mere teen, could I, cruising Chicago,

Hear your siren's call and steal you away
From your parents' house, yet a little girl.

AND what a miracle that our future is intact
Even though you lost your way and I mine
Enduring years of wide co-wanderings.
Yet God's sure Hand held us, turned us round,
Our eyes bound, as in a children's game
Of blindman's bluff, then suddenly the blinds—
Off! Ripped from our amazed disoriented eyes.
Ah! You! Fascinating!
Ah! What an endless revelation!

AND here we are, miraculously, celebrating
Eighteen real, incredible, enviable years.
You see me, still, you say, as some kind
Of Adonis, and I know you every day
As my Venus incarnate. Our eyes
Drink one another in, glistening
Tearing; our lips curl into a smile.
Our bodies like sympathetic bells vibrate
When we near one another, our arms
Reach out to embrace, our noses sniff,
Our fingers explore one another's flesh.

V

Sure, we will carry in us always
Looking back, a wistful "IF ONLY"
With its correlative "THEN" and reflexive "BUT"
But most of all, my beauty, we will live
Every day our expansive "AND".
Your hand holds my hand now, your heart
Cradles mine, your voice sings
In perfect harmony with mine
While we harvest our pleasures today.

We are not bound down by conditional clauses,
By "ifs" and "thens", or by traditional tenses.
As our past is present, so is the future now.

We are not merely recalling "I loved you then"
Nor wishing for tomorrow "I will love you when".
But in the present, in this very moment,
On a peak eighteen miles high,
Toward heaven and forever, we are bold to say:

"Tomorrow I am loving you; I love you today."

BLESSINGS FAR AND NEAR

When I was 9 and you were far
(But not so far),
Away,
I spent my day
Half in school and half in play.

My mind and soul ran everywhere,
Bemused, in prayer;
Each day
I would wake and say,
"What am I doing here, anyway?"

I did not know that you were sitting,
Like a perked up kitten
Or a dove
In God's gloved
Hand, searching earth for your love.

You were poised to skip through heaven's gate
To become my fate,
Glad if
I would have it,
And not hop off like a scared jackrabbit.

When you were 1 and I was one
Thousand (some)
Miles
Away, my smiles
Showed I was a captive to your childlike wiles

But I was dumb as any dog
Or frog or log
When I
(In Chi) drove by--
A boy who did not hear you sigh (or cry).

Angels must have flown you round
In New York town.
Oh, fie!
My blinded eye
Missed the vision. How could I?

When there on Goethe Street you walked,
I should have gawked
To see
The one for me.
No--played pure comedy.

You too graced the sit-com stage--
We'd skip a page,
A scene,
What could it mean?
That things are seldom what they seem?

Then one day our lives would flower
In the English tower
When you
Stopped by on cue
To ask me what I thought you should do.

Ha!

Of course, become my home, my pearl
Of great price girl,
The goal--
The hole in my soul
I'll have to fill up to be made whole.

You were near and yet so far away--
Every day,
A student
Whom I couldn't
Forget was drop-dead gorgeous (though it doesn't rhyme
with student).

But then you were gone--so far, so far
An impossible star.
Space
Separated us. By grace
In my heart, I held your face.

The angels swirled, the stars tumbled
Our lives stumbled
On.
Then a new dawn
Riveted our eyes on a rising sun.

We shot our arrows into the air
Then suddenly, there
You were
Our hearts were astir
That I was the him and you were the her.

I was the one and you were the only
Neither of us lonely
Now.
Ready to vow
Our lives away like puppies: Bow wow!

Now each night you are for me my sweet
Beneath my sheet.
I taste
Daily and feast
On your flesh, no deliciouser treat.

And I pray, my sassy little girl
With sassy curl,
That you
Find me for you
As overwhelming a blessing as I do you.

TWENTY QUICK AND QUIRKY YEARS

(THEN TWENTY MORE?)

(A NON-SONNET)

20 YEARS—it ain't a big deal--

We're still just a couple of untrained seals

Who laugh like loons and fight like cats,

Playful in pleasure, then exploding in spats

That leave us near dead. It's a dangerous game—

To cuddle and coo, then blow up in blame.

Our passions we never apparently have mastered,

Though our love is intense, our anger's a disaster.

After years together, can't we figure it out--

How to live our love, or what love's all about?

Do we have 20 more? Only God can say.

But we can try to live each precious day

As if it were our last, or, perhaps, just one

Grand prize in a lotto we've won.

Twenty Little Things

I

Sure, I could spin you a eulogy about
Twenty big things (there are more, no doubt),
That fascinate me about you: your face,
Your ass, your legs, the musical grace
Of your dancing bod, your spirit, your heart--
Things that mesmerized me from the start
And caused my mouth to gape, my soul
To yearn that you be mine.

                    Your whole
Self—your extraordinary energy, your tact,
Your sensuousness—overwhelmed me, in fact,
And your language and memory, emotional intensity,
Your penchant for fun, your health, the density
Of your thought, your probing mind, your key
Choice to share your life with me.
I love the way the curves in you
Soften my angles, and your woman's view
Opens my male mind. We share
Song and dance, drama, dining, and dare
To travel to far, strange lands.

                    In twenty
Years, we managed to see our world a-plenty.
You sharing yourself and your life with me
Is the biggest thing that's happened to me--
Ever.

      Oh, for twenty big things I could easily
Focus on your fabulous face, and breezily
Laud your nose, chin, and luscious lips,
Your coy smile between tiny sips
Of our evening "toon", your enticing smile,

Your pomegranate cheeks, your utter guile-
lessness, simplicity in significant looks
That you learned from life and not from books.

I could go on about these huge matters
That cause my heart many pitters and patters:
I could speak of the firmness of your expressive ass
Or the epithetical appropriateness of your creative sass.
I could rave about your shoulders, muscular, round,
That I love to nibble on, before working down
To your perfect boozie, steamy torso,
Which I could go on kissing for an hour or so.

But I love as well the wellspring of laughter
That peppers your discourse, and then, after
We've chatted at the end of work, the way
You rise to the music and lead me to sway
Rhythmically with you to Parios' croon,
As if we were romancing out under the moon.
I love to look at your fetching stance
Whether contemplating dinner or preparing to dance.
I am awed by your salmon, the chicken you bake—
Better than the best city chefs could make!

You deserve my recognition for all you do
To gain for us a first-rate reservation to
A restaurant, hotel, a drama, a cruise—
Events that fulfill our dreams or amuse
Our hearts. We drink in one another
When at our amusements we are aware
Of how precious it is: this life we share.

II

These more-than-twenty reflected delights
I could expound and develop, but my sights
Have landed elsewhere today: on diggies!

Not the same, no, no, as fairy-tale piggies
But twenty little diggies dancing about--
Playful or stern, curling up, stretching out--
To which my eye is easily drawn.
Each little diggie can easily spawn
In me a little poem, at least one line
(For every little thing of yours is mine).
I've drunk you in, you are a part of me,
And these little diggies, as you will see,
I have assimilated. They are yours, but I, too,
Claim them as gifts that I have from you.

The twenty little items I'm meditating on
Are at the end of your feet and the end of each arm.
Ten are above and ten are below
All are arranged artistically in rows.
On two sexy hands, ten sexy fingers
(When you're out of eyesight, the image still lingers).
Ten sexy toes on two sexy feet
(I want to kiss them, they're utterly sweet!)
Ten on the left and ten on the right
(Whatever side I'm on, I get full sight).
You offer twenty diggies to meditate on:
I can view them all together, or take them one by one.

III

Let's start with the littlest diggie on your
Right hand—straight as an arrow, pure
As silk, funny like a clown, active
Without any sense of the huge impact it
Makes on me when I watch it twirl
And say to myself, "Ah, that's my girl!"

The littlest diggie on your left hand boasts
Similar traits, but also hosts
Sophisticated movements, such as

To extend itself and rise up straight
To signal approval or to indicate
Hesitation or meditation
About a play, a taste, a medication
For which some doubt has crept into
Your mind that you had never meant to
Entertain. Whether you'll be rigid
Or cool, you express in this firm digit.

On each of your feet are five cute diggies
That remind the child in us of little piggies--
One went to market, one stayed home,
One ate roast beef, one ate none,
And one cried "Wee, wee". Why? we query,
But asking why can only make us weary.
On each of your feet, your five fine diggies
Are nothing at all like the tale's five piggies.
When one goes to Dominick's, all go along
Like chorus members singing a song.
Whether right five or left, when the foot stays home
All the little diggies string right along.
But when, with your legs tucked beneath, you pose
On the couch, sipping in peaceful repose,
Each of your diggies makes a speech of its own—
With cheerful chuckle or a world-weary groan.
One twitters on with a rhythm subdued,
Another beats boldly a tune: "I love you."
The littlest diggie laughs but makes no noise
And the others laugh too, but without any voice.
Together they put on a rhythmic play
Just for me, just to hear me say
To you, my beloved, how much I delight
In the music your body creates tonight.

I cannot forget the other hand-diggies
I left up above when I turned to the "piggies."
They have no names, like "Blitzen " or "Donder"
Or "Silver" or "Lassie", but they do wonders
Almost without lifting a fing-

er. A left one is usually sporting a ring.
A right one, punching keys, sends words
Through a computer, faster than birds
Could carry your message. When you pluck
Your cuisine from a skillet, you usually suck
One of those diggies on your coated right hand.
Mmm, what delicious! With your thumb
And index, you can pinch an arm till it's numb,
Or seize some salt to throw in the pot
Or send God's healing to a troubled spot
On my pained body. At night, abed,
Your reach out your right to caress my head.
Then they work together, the righthand five,
To convince me, though tired, I'm still alive.
One fondles my sideburn, one tousles my hair,
One strokes my cheek, one tickles my ear.
I don't know what the fifth one is doing
But I know I am pleased and I feel like cooing.

Sometimes you come to stand behind me,
You wrap your arms round, and your diggies find me
Awaiting their exploration. They
Trace my contours, dance and play
On my bosom, trip down my nips,
Circle my stomach and land on my hips.
I cannot say I find it annoying;
In fact, you seem to know I'm enjoying
Your little diggie game. And I am!
If ever I suppress my emotions or dam
Up my feelings, your diggies dig
Them out of me. A very big
Job for such little creatures! But
If I didn't give thanks, I'd be a big nut.

IV

So those are some of the reasons why
I turned to your twenty diggies, to try
To honor their contribution today
When we celebrate twenty years to the day
Since first we exchanged our heartfelt "I do's"
In public ceremony. You are my muse
And have always been. Whatever I write
Stems from loving you, and the sight
Of your glorious flesh, from head to toe,
And those twenty diggies, ten in each row.

In Santorini

YES, I LOVE HER

"Yes, I love her," I tell the page
Staring blankly back at me. "And
After all, another year has passed,
And we, still together, know we could
Never be apart, not for a night."

"What is there about her," I ask,
"That makes a year go by, as if
It were merely a moment?" The page
Pretends to be a teacher, or preciser,
A psychiatrist, and counters:
"You say?"

"Absorption?" I ask myself. "Do I
So wrap around her shape, fascinated
By her beauty, by her raw emotions,
That all my sensitivities explode, so that
Time can't squeeze its way into my
Consciousness?" At seven we sip
Our "toon," talking, touching. At nine,
We suddenly find time passed
Without passing at all!

"What is there," I ask, "about her cheeks
That make me unaware that the sun
Is setting?" The page stares blankly back:
"Tell me."

"Her cheeks shine," I say, "like two suns:
One brightly rising, one sensuously setting."
It is neither morning nor evening, but both
Together, so time stands still, stupefied,
Not knowing which way to go, or goes
Backward while I gaze, fascinated, rapt,
Timelessly contemplating eternal beauty.

"But" suggests the blank page,
"What about emptiness." "Oh!"
I respond. "When she goes away,
When a tiff creates a slammed door,
An empty chair, silence-- then
There is nothing for me but waiting,
Endless waiting, where each second
Is at least an hour, more likely a day,
A year-- forever. The sun doesn't rise,
And, always, sleep is hours away."

"And?" asks the empty blank sheet
Under my pen. "But," I write, "not 'and'."
BUT the night can move along, and sleep
Can engulf us as soon as the emotional
Storm yields to her acquiescent smile,
And our bodies intervene to teach us
The touches that turn time on again,
And make time sleep in our wrapped-up
Quiescent limbs.

"Do you contradict yourself?" "Of course.
How can I not? How can I cry,
'She loves me!' without whispering in my soul,
'She loves me not!'" Time stops, time runs,
Life stops, life runs on jubilantly,
Peacefully, raucously, madly, insanely.

"Twenty-one: what does that mean
To you, to her?" "Nothing," I say,
"It doesn't matter. We 'were'
Before the universe was there to catch us,
We 'are' long after earth has spun away
Off into space, a flash, forgotten
Even by aliens who may have been
Conscious of its departure."

"And time?" "Will be no more." I
Will be lost in her face, her cheeks,
Her smile, her voice, her arms, her whole
Musical body. And we, each moment forever
Will be wrapped up and lost
And found in one another's arms.

V

SPECIAL LOVE DAYS
IN ORDINARY TIME

Throughout the Year

Valentine Poems

True lovers experience their love every day of the year. But there are numerous ways that lovers express that love, reflect on it, highlight its uniqueness, exalt in it, imagine it ("Two Thousand Eleven Reasons"). Many lovers are excited by receiving a picture of a heart on Valentine Day, along with a personal message from the beloved ("My Heart"). Some find the sentiments in such cards to be shallow, and so create their own personalized message for their lover ("A Private Place"). Read the "Valentine Day Poems."

Everyday Anyday Poems

A simple kiss can be a powerful profession of love ("Our Come-Home-Everyday Kiss"). So is a rose ("Roses Are Red, Are They?"), a garden ("Private Garden"), a breeze ("Breeze on Your Breasts"), a bump ("Bump on Your Buttocks). A lover often thinks of devouring the object of his passions ("Degustation: A Deconstructive View of a Delicious Babe"). These images rise in the imagination at whim, during "ordinary time". Read the "Everyday Anyday Poems."

Special Love Days in Ordinary Time

<u>Valentine's Day</u>

A Private Place
Valentine
My Heart
Earth, Sky, and Sea
February
Two Thousand Eleven Reasons

<u>Everyday Anyday</u>

Our Come-Home-Everyday Kiss
Private Garden
Every Day
Addict
The Edge of Things
My Annie
Growing Young
Breeze on Your Breasts
Bump on Your Buttocks
Roses Are Red, Are They?
What's Not to Love
Degustation: A Deconstructive View of a Delicious Babe

Statue and Heart

A PRIVATE PLACE

For tradesmen, Valentine is but an enterprise

when crimson candy boxes sneak into stores

conspiring with heart-shaped greeting cards galore

and rose-bouquets. Bought gifts epitomize

heart's warmth. Can sparkling diamonds symbolize

depth of feeling, with their polished cold hard core?

If fire is in them, is it not so even more

in hands, words, lips, looks, sighs?

Engulfed by crass displays on every side,

we balk to bend our souls to the lock-step dance,

avoid crowded venues, the public race.

Daily in our hearts' hearthfire, we reside

in a private place. There, in perennial trance,

we eat each other and our hearts embrace.

Valentine

What does this guy named Val-
entine have to do with my love?
Does he cheerlead the sexes to ral-
ly, cooing like lovey-doves?

Can he make a Sam or a Sal-
ly suddenly burn with romance?
Or teach a clueless Gal-
lant how to romantically dance?

Stores go on promoting the fal-
acy that a val-card can alter your life,
but if the card's greeting is mal-
apropos, instead it can generate strife.

My lover is not just my pal
to accompany me to a show,
she's my heart, my intrigue, my cal-
ypso, the light that makes me glow.

In two hundred seven, Saint Val-
entine bit the proverbial dust.
He may never have fucked his gal,
His love-life was likely a bust.

His breath may have been mal-
odorous, his hugging may have been weak,
he may have wandered in a val-
ley of ignorance, or even been a freak!

But you and I are called Val-
entines; so, OK, just let it be.
I love you true, and you, my gal,
You, I swear, love me.

My Heart

There are nuMerous ways you thrill me,

you, the One, the OnlY love of my life! Your face lights

my days; just to be tHinking of you gives me such joy;

then, when we are togEther, hearing your resonant voice

warms me, your Arms around me comfort me

your fine fingeRs caressing my sideburns

say "You're iT! My heart's heart!"

EARTH, SKY, AND SEA

Since I love you as you love me,
We give each other: EARTH, SKY, and SEA,
And trinkets to look at and fine clothes to wear,
Morsels to munch on, moments to share.

Our legs, entwined, dance all night long,
The words we speak are Love's Sweet Song.
Our shouts of pleasure, our intense embrace,
The fierceness of our kisses, give Love a face.

And the thousand kindnesses we daily bestow
On one another are Love's dumbshow:
Trash taken out, piles of bills paid,
Travel arrangements, sandwiches made,

Rising at dawn, ruling all day
Our respective realms, as one might say,
To put funds in the bank, ideas in the head,
Fine food on the table, fresh sheets on the bed.

You and I, Love, in a romantic trance
Image the Archetypical Lovers' Dance.
Swirling to waltzes or a Parios tune
Like frolicking elves under a lunatic moon.

So we take from God who freely bestows
A world and a way where our Love grows.
So I take from you, and you from me
God's Valentine gift: EARTH, SKY, and SEA.

FEBRUARY

It's winter
        And

    we just made love

And

      your silk sinewy body
      breathes next to mine
      your face like a meadow
      your arms warm around me

And I

      though some suppose declining
      reclining thrilled and filled
      in the room of your aromas
      in the bath of your beauty
      in the sureness of your smile

And

      harsh words evaporate like dew
      on a new morning; I no longer recall
      my philosophy of idiocy nor you
      your theology of rightful wrath

  See

      the frozen lake outside our window
      already thawing, its icehard surface
      dancing to the tides' rhythms
      if only for this one winter's night

See

      the stars shut their mouths and move on
      after pausing in their orbits to hearken
      to our laughter that shook the heavens
      a moment of eternal ecstasy

Ah
    I feel reaching through the stars
    the hot touch of God that gave me you
    and you me to play together
    warm in this chilly garden,
    this February night

Sooke Harbor Sailor Girl

TWO THOUSAND ELEVEN REASONS

I
only
have
2011
this year
(so far)
but
next year
(I feel)
I'll have
many
more

2012
(at least).

No,
don't fear!
I'm not
going
to spell
them
all out
here.

2012
(that's a lot!)

Here's but a
hasty
tasting
of reasons
this season
that I can't
live without

(you know,
there's no doubt
who)

you!

It's no duty
to love your beauty—
my story's
to love your astounding glory.
Your glowing eyes
are my daily prize,
and every sip
from your luscious lips
thrills me. I seek
to kiss each cheek
as often as I may.
And I cannot say
enough about
your sexy mouth,
and that perfect chin—
tell me when
I'll see another such.

Further
That flicking finger,
the little finger
with a mind of its own,
as if alone
it dances around
without a sound.
But the others,
its brothers,
know how to rustle,
massage, & tousle
my hair, electrify
the flesh near my eye
or my nips

or my lips
or smooth my hair.
And with what care
and gentleness your hand
traverses the land
of my shoulders and chest,
and with what zest
caresses my ass
or makes a pass
at my privates. Yow!
So much for now
about your hand!
There's not sand
enough in an hour-
glass to tell the power
of your laugh--how the spell
of it rings my bell!
Your sexy voice
entices me. My choice
is yield or die!
I love to eye
your perfect shoulders,
which, like soldiers,
muscled and strong,
guard you all day long.
Your voluminous hair
tempts the air
to play in it, then cause
the curls to pause,
to assume a design
so gorgeous and so fine
that my heart weeps
while my eye keeps
tracing the ring-
lets and my soul sings.

Bosoms you have two:
each one I woo

with my eager kiss.
But I must not miss
your silken torso.
Then an hour or so
I must expend
handling that end
of you they call
the "rear." Of all
women, I vow,
there's none, now
nor never, could boast,
she had the most
firm, fit,
bounteous bit
of bottom. No,
you own the show!

I must make a case
for your sticking place:
splendid, magnifique!
Elegant and chic!
And not all that chaste.
But I must haste
on to your danc-
er's legs. In pants
or skirt, you show
me music: your toe
always ready
to dance, ready
to twirl me round.
In your body, the sound
of music is al-
ways playing—I am in awe
when you walk
rhythmically, talk
rhythmically.
I swoon when I see
you move from sink to oven.

Your tongue,
Your teeth, your knees,
the gentle breeze
of your breath—I can
not name the pan-
oply of all
the graces that you call
your body. Just know,
I love you so!

I wish I had time
to tell you in rhyme
the items I left
out. I'm not so deft
as to make a poem
out of all in our home
you do to make
us happy. I'll take
a shot to say
that you, every day,
give love deep meaning
by cooking and cleaning
and manning the station
to make reservations,
tending the flowers
to give them new powers
of pleasure promotion;
analyzing notions
conveyed on the news
and airing your views;
stimulating life
in me, resolving strife,
greeting with a smile,
loving without guile:
Me.
Don't you see?

Here, take this clue:
that means that you

are sure mine
own
true
Valentine.

No Duty to Love Beauty

Our Come-Home-Everyday Kiss

My key clicks in the Lock. Seven o'clock.

I hear your bare feet running on dancer's legs.

Our bloods call to one another through the peephole.

I see already your apple cheeks like two suns

Rising above the sudden sunburst of your exploding

Smile. The door falls away like an apparition

To reveal the reality that is you. And suddenly

Our mouths, like the horses in Macbeth,

Are eating one another, sucking on one another's

souls for sustenance and the sense of being

Alive. My cheeks, my chin, my whole face

Are emptied into the surging liposuctive vortex

Of your all-demanding bilabial devouring.

My lips and nose, after feasting on your face,

Nuzzle into your succulent neck. My teeth find

The meat of your neck, the fruit of your ear,

Tastier than nectar. My tongue licks the natural

Sugar from your berry-ripe breasts. Then we hear

The music playing – be it Bach's Brandenburgs

Or Horwitz's Mozart concerti, or Yanni's Moog.

We are swept away, like Chagall's

Flying and kissing lovers, circling

The swirling sun in ecstatic whoops

And whirls. And magically, we are home.

PRIVATE GARDEN

Propped on our love seat couch,
Surrounded by green things growing,
We joy in one another's hearts,
Sip Bombay Sapphire martinis and, in love,
Nibble pretzels, almonds, fingertips,
The healthy spiciness of multi-graced living.

Too long have the hours held our bodies,
Like magnets straining toward perfect union,
Apart. Now, lost in each other's gaze,
We hear, as distant reverberations, our voices,
The clean piping of a native Indian soul-song.

Blessed by ivies and jades, we are attended
By angelic dieffenbachias, ficuses, and ferns,
The Song of India, the Chinese evergreen,
Norfolk pine, two-trunked rubber tree,
The three-in-one croton on oriental base
And occasional bursts of red and white roses.

Yet we carry our Eden with us where we go.
It knows storms, terrors, invasions, wars,
But God gave us gates no intruder may enter
Where we, embowered in our green-growing love,
Know nothing but the paradoxical peace and deep
Excitement of loving, the blessing of God.

EVERY DAY

Every day I write to you
My muse, my beauty.
Our love wakes words in me
Strong and true.

Green things grow in my head
As under your thumb
And sprout on the note-pad page
Under my fondling finger.

The allure of your flesh, deep, fresh,
Silky succulent skin
The aroma of a field of fascinating fragrances:
My nose knows it's you.

I adore you with the waking sun,
With the heat-incensing early afternoon,
In a long lingering going of the last light
In the glory of a star-bedazzled night.

ADDICT

I am addicted to you
Day or night
The very sight of you
Hooks me.

I sip your face, one sip
The taste of your eyes in my throat
Sears my veins sensuously
Euphoria eases the nerves in my neck.

I swill my tongue around your lips
A tingling sets off bells of rejoicing
Through the temple of my desires
Knelling unending celebration.

In my head, I have already seized
With my lion's jaw your brazen ass,
Fondly recalling the jungle chase
The bounce of your meaty cheeks.

I feed on you, drooling;
My blood becomes a lazy river
Poppy-strewn, and my heart's pleasure's roar
Scares off all noises in my meddlesome brain.

My Addiction

THE EDGE OF THINGS

We hold one another trembling

on this ball swirling through space.

Your right hand hats my head

to protect my naked pate

against attacks of time and hate.

I press your dancer's body

against my chest, my nose nuzzling

your aromatic neck. I need you

safe against nightmares and pain.

We stand on the edge of things,

thankful, afraid. It is day

but night lingers on the horizon.

It is night, but day will dawn.

MY ANNIE

I have a little girl.
Her head is full of curls
Bountiful and beauteous
And malleable.

When she is good
She is very, very good,
So when she is bad,
It is tolerable.

Tolerable

GROWING YOUNG

Though I grow old
Your favors grow me young
Whether you hand them me
With hand
Or tell them me
With tongue.

Mistress of favors, this
I know:
When you contrive that
I young grow,
Each hand or tongue
You gift to me
Or tightness you secure
(Moist and tingly
Swallowing me up)
Makes you, like me
Grow younger too
Younger, much younger
than me.

BREEZE ON YOUR BREASTS

I am the whisper of a wild wind
Whistling your attention to me.
You hear, harken, look round,
But no, no one, it appears, is near.

But that's my airy hand
Fluffing your bountiful sexy tresses.
You sit in the shade of a cedar
And feel something, my breath, on your cheeks.

You suck in air, and, over your lips,
My unsubstantial tongue touches yours.

I see you stretched in the sun--
Who is that you feel caressing
Your bikini-clad body, your fulsome breasts
Half covered by a skimpy bra?

Imagine me and know it's true.

BUMP ON YOUR BUTTOCKS

I am the body of a mad mind
Mad for your body, driven
Insane by your whipped cream
Flesh. Whose hand caresses

Your hot thighs, fluffs
Your bountiful sexy tresses?
Even with eyes closed, you know.
Whose breath warms your cheeks.

Your lips welcome mine, our tongues
Play pat-a-cake, our juices combine.

My fingers tickle your nip tips
And stir your hot spot. You shiver
As I, shivering as well, mount you.
We lose ourselves in ecstasy.

Imagine me and know it's true!

ROSES ARE RED, ARE THEY?

Roses are red, violets are blue,
Truffle's delicious, and so are you.

A rose, it is said, a rose, dear, is red
But what tint have the roses we find in the bed?

Red, yes, but also: white, yellow, and pink--
More colors by far than most people think!

But what about violets, violets are blue?
You'd think they'd be violet, would not you?

So must we accept that roses are red
And forget all the other roses in the bed?

And must we accept that violets are blue
And act like we're dumb and we haven't a clue?

I say that roses are red, white, and blue
And I say that violets are violet, too.

So call me a radical, call me a clown,
Or call me a prophet, talk of the town.

No matter what I say, you'll know this is true:
Some roses are red and I love you.

Lovers, Mountains, Sea, & Sky

WHAT'S NOT TO LOVE

We clean the house
We play some Scrabble
I empty the trash
We fry frittatas

You reserve hotels
You plan some trips
We sip our tunes
We kiss our lips

We fly to Rome
We visit Greece
We hike Alaska
We roam 'round Nice

We shop at Dominick's
We shop Whole Foods
You create "cuisine"
That trumps mere "good"

You come to bed
(Where I've hit the hay)
Our bodies blend
In a luscious way

There's lots, lots more
Every God-blessed day
We inhabit our island
A great place to stay!

Degustation:
A Deconstructive View of a Delicious Babe

Anticipation

That you are near:
A sense of sun in a still dark dawn
A thrill in the spine at the top of a hill
Overlooking lush orchards, a whiff
Of ginger and cumin on the wind

Eye on the Prize

You come into view:
Immeasurably pleasurable proportionality
Curvaceous contours of mountainous Provence
Pursed lusciousness of liquid lips
Pedestaled goddess of crafty Milo

Nose in the Neck

As we squeeze one another in greeting:
Rosemary pinched on a garden walk
Garlic and olive oil in fresh-cut tomatoes
Desert blooms in bunches on a bench for two
Pork chops sizzling in a vegetable broth

Memory of Music

As I drink in your movements:
Parios and Demetra haunt the mind
Bocelli's crescendos swell wave after wave
And Marc Antony's driving calypso rhythms
Are stored in your hips, your taut calves

Picasso's Head

I deconstruct your facial features:
Circle smothered in curly-cue curls
Or, elegant elongations ending at chinpoint
Mystical mountains bulge in your cheeks
Shining planets swirl in your eyes

Four Ways to Look at Your Feet

I love your feet in myriad presentations:
Kitchen: Bare blessings of sushi-quality flesh
Bedroom: Smothered in a floppy stocking ragout
Outdoors: Tooling along trussed up in sneakers
On the town: Sizzling in 4-inch pointy-toed heels

Pièce de Résistance

You the main course, multi-flavored you:
Lips sip lips, savory, perfect
Your spicy saliva, I gulp down greedily,
Lips lick nips, fine buttery bread
I devour your puss, compliments to the chef!

And For Dessert

We lie along one another:
The sweep of your hand over my torso
Light in the eyes, sly smiling, sweet
Not saccharine, like dark chocolate three ways
Long lingering tastes on satisfied palates

Endless Pleasure

You are all the foods in my daily diet:
I know I have come to the right establishment
Exquisite décor, perfection of service,
Hot foods hot, cold foods chilled
Confident kicked-up stunning seasoning

EPILOGUE

"Read Me Your Kisses"

The Gift

Read Me Your Kisses

When you said to me, "Read me your kisses,"
I opened *Love's Liturgy* and there they were!

We laughed through "Ear Tickle," our lips all a-tingle
Swelling to a pucker as we wandered through it.

My songs kissed your "FACE—the Music of It"
My smile kissed your curls in the sandbox scene.

We licked our chops through "Degustation"
We sucked our souls as we enjoyed the feast.

I lay before you "Twenty Little Things"
And in verse nibbled each delectable diggie.

My tongue articulated your indescribable beauty,
Your face, your body, your mind, your soul.

My words were a breeze on your bountiful breasts
Each sound a rose, either violet or red.

Clothed only in words we embraced in Eden,
Our Private Garden, so Green and Golden.

Each poem, my beloved, each whistle of you
Each word of wonderment is a smackeroo.

Each verse, each kiss, is a Jewel of the Heart,
How rich we become, bedecked in these diamonds!

So whether I am near you, or far, far away,
I can always kiss you, your face and your heart

By tickling your ear with an urgent command:
"Open *Love's Liturgy* and read my lips!"

CPSIA information can be obtained at www.ICGtesting.com
Printed in the USA
LVOW112006150212

268917LV00001B/5/P